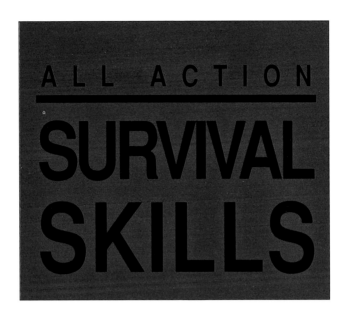

ALL ACTION
SURVIVAL SKILLS

LIBBY ROBERTS

LERNER PUBLICATIONS COMPANY
MINNEAPOLIS

Titles in this series

Backpacking
Climbing
Kayacking
Mountain Biking
Skateboarding
Skiing
Survival Skills
Wind and Surf

Photographs are reproduced by permission of the following: pp. 11, 15, 39, 40, 41, 43, Eye Ubiquitous; pp. 35 (main picture), 36, 37, Phil Holden; p. 23, Jimmy Holmes; pp. 4, 7, 8, 16, 19 (top), 24, Brian Litz; pp. 14 (bottom), 20, 21, 22, Mountin' Excitement/Donoghue; pp. 9, 14, 35 (inset), Christine Osborne; pp. 6, 26, 32 (bottom), 33, 42, Photri; p. 32 (top), Tony Stone Worldwide/Tim Brown; p. 18, Tony Stone Worldwide/Steve Chimpson; p. 5, Tony Stone Worldwide/Mark Lewis; p. 28, Tony Stone Worldwide/Bob Martin; p. 38, Tony Stone Worldwide/David Patterson; p. 13, Tony Stone Worldwide/Yamada Toshiro; p. 25, Tony Stone Worldwide/Karl Weatherly; pp. 29, 30, Tickle Group; p. 12, Trails Illustrated. All artwork by Steve Wheele.

First published in the United States in 1993
by Lerner Publications Company

Copyright © 1992 by Wayland (Publishers) Limited
First published in 1992 by Wayland (Publishers) Ltd
61 Western Rd, Hove, East Sussex BN3 1JD, England

Library of Congress Cataloging-in-Publication Data
Roberts, Libby
        Survival skills / Libby Roberts.
            p.   cm. — (All action)
        Includes bibliographical references and index.
        Summary: Discusses how to avoid danger and deal with emergencies
    in the wilderness, on the beach, and in the city.
        ISBN 0-8225-2481-3
        1. Survival skills—Juvenile literature. 2. Wilderness survival—
    Juvenile literature. [1. Survival. 2. Safety.] I. Title. II. Series.
        GF86.R63   1993
        613.6'9—dc20   92-800
                                                                      CIP
                                                                       AC

Printed in Italy
Bound in the United States of America
1 2 3 4 5 6 7 8 9 10 02 01 00 99 98 97 96 95 94 93

Contents

Adventure sports always carry the risk of injury. By practicing proper safety precautions, you can reduce your risk of getting hurt. This book will give you some ideas about participating safely in adventure sports, but there isn't really any substitute for taking classes and getting safety training from experts.

INTRODUCTION

Have you ever picked up a survival book in a bookstore before? If you have, you probably noticed that they teach you how to get along in the wilderness when you can't get back to safety. They show you how to skin rabbits and make fires from whatever materials are available. To survive, you don't really need to know how to skin a rabbit — or how to catch one in the first place.

Instead of having to catch and skin a rabbit, wouldn't you rather have taken some food with you in the first place? This book will teach you to anticipate when something could go wrong and how to prevent a problem before it even arises. So if you wanted to find out how to light a fire using a moldy old sock or how to skin a snake with your teeth, you should find one of those other survival books. However, if you want to learn how to make your outdoor adventure safe and practical, keep reading.

The idea of this book is to suggest safe ways of taking part in potentially dangerous sports. We won't discuss games like soccer, football, basketball, or hockey, although these can be dangerous.

RIGHT

Camping in the hills takes you into beautiful country. But make sure that you are prepared for any problems that might come up.

LEFT

It's much easier to heat up some pasta than to catch and skin a rabbit!

Instead, we will discuss sports like hiking, kayaking, and ocean swimming. Part of the fun of these sports is that they can get you away from everyday life. While you're hiking or kayaking, you won't have anyone asking, "Have you done your homework yet?" or "What do you want to be when you grow up?" People do not usually ask these questions halfway up a mountain or in the middle of a fast-flowing river.

Away from routine, everyday worries, you can enjoy the challenge of making sure that you will make it back to your **campsite** before the sun goes down. But every challenge carries risks. There are problems with being away from the everyday world; you are far from things like

Weather

Whenever you can, check the weather forecast for the days of your trip. This will help you decide what equipment to take with you. If the forecast calls for a weeklong heat wave, you won't need to take much extra warm clothing. Long-range weather forecasts give you some idea of what to expect for your trip, but the most useful forecasts are for the day ahead.

ambulances, hospitals, and warm beds that you can snuggle down into if you feel cold and tired.

Always try to remember this: Out in the wilderness, you are unlikely to get quick help from someone else. It may come, but you can never rely on it. You will be much better off if you figure out beforehand exactly what might happen in any circumstances and be ready.

Throughout this book there is a lot of advice on how to deal with dangerous situations. But you should learn how to recognize possible danger in advance. Avoiding danger is better than having to get out of it. Even very smart people can have trouble thinking clearly when dealing with the pressure of a hazardous situation. Always try to think ahead and predict what might go wrong.

White-water kayakers have a saying: "Less than three should never be." In fact, when taking part in a dangerous sport, you should try to have at least four people in your group. Fewer than three people are not likely to be able to get themselves out of difficulty. If someone is injured, for example, at least one person should stay with her or him, while someone else goes for help.

As a rule, it is a bad idea to go out

in a group of more than six. This is because when there are a lot of people, someone who gets separated from the group is less likely to be noticed as missing. If there are, say, nine people in your group, divide into three groups of three, or one group of five and one of four. Make sure that the more experienced people are spread between the groups so that they can help the less experienced people.

Always decide on a group coordinator for each outing, preferably the most experienced person in the group. The coordinator's job isn't to tell everyone what to do. It's to plan a route and also to find out what people think about a situation

RIGHT

Always go hiking with a group of other people, so you can help each other in an emergency.

Reading maps

In any activity that involves going to places where there are no road signs or marked paths, you must be able to read maps and use a compass. Most hiking books will explain how to read maps and use compasses. Just reading books isn't enough, though. You will need to practice before you go to an unfamiliar place.

and then try to help everyone decide what to do.

For example, you might be out walking in the mountains. Ahead of you is a patch of slippery ground with a steep drop on one side. There may be one person in your group who challenges everyone to cross it, while another person may be scared at the thought of having to cross. The coordinator's job is to find out how confident each person is about his or her ability to cross. If even one person doesn't think he or she can make it, the coordinator should find an alternate route or lead your group back the way you came.

Never let the group split up. If it does, a part of your potential rescue team has been lost. If you are traveling in a group of three that splits up, one person will be out alone. (There is advice on how to find a lost group member on pages 20 and 21.)

Finally, whatever you are doing, make sure that you have the right equipment with you. Sometimes it is hard to tell whether a piece of equipment is really necessary or is just expensive junk. Colored boxes in each chapter show the essential

ABOVE

Make sure that you're properly equipped. These white-water rafters in Indonesia have helmets and life jackets.

equipment you should have. Some of it is the same for different sports.

In whatever activity you pursue, these ideas about working as a group and looking ahead for potential trouble should be remembered. They will make things safer and a lot more fun.

Even after you have read this book, don't think you can immediately lead a group out into the wilderness. It would be very dangerous for all of you. Safety is learned through experience, and the best place for you to get experience is with a qualified instructor.

DESERTS

D eserts are famous for their hot winds and sandstorms. I had always thought of deserts as being completely dry — just miles of heat and dust. I thought there might be a few cacti, some scorpions crawling around, and maybe a snake or two slithering in the sand.

Storm warnings

Never camp in a dried-up riverbed, no matter how calm the weather seems. You never know what the weather is doing several miles away from you, or if there is snow melting just behind the next ridge. Look for a place above the highest waterline.

If lightning strikes, remember that the tops of hills are most likely to be hit. Keep your distance from tall objects, but don't become the tallest object around either. Many injuries caused by lightning are from electric currents that travel through the ground near the lightning strike. Do not shelter in cracks in the rock or under shallow overhangs, because the current can flow through and across the openings of these. A spacious cave, at least 10 feet (more than three m) high and wide, is quite safe if you stay away from the walls.

LEFT

Take the proper precautions to protect yourself in electrical storms.

I realized how wrong I'd been as Mary, Elvis, and I ran for the shelter of a large cave in the desert canyons south of the Canyonlands National Park in Utah. "I'm glad we brought our rain gear!" I shouted over the downpour. Sheets of water were rushing off a nearby ledge. We sat there watching the storm.

Elvis shed his backpack and pulled out a plastic bag of nuts and dried fruit. We munched on the food as we watched the spectacular lightning flashes. "Hey, look out!" A lightning bolt struck a tall red sandstone pillar about 30 feet (10 meters) to the right of our shelter.

We could barely see where the sun was behind the rainclouds, but our watches told us that we had about two hours of daylight left. We decided to stay where we were for the night. We seemed unlikely to find anywhere more comfortable. Our shelter was several feet higher than the desert floor and at least 350 feet (107 m) from the dried-up riverbed we had spotted earlier, so it was a safe place to sleep.

Mary pulled out our **topographical maps** and **time-control plan** (our plan for how much ground we

would cover each day), to check our schedule. "We're doing fine," she said. "We should get to the north end of Fable Valley tomorrow afternoon."

Mary and I had planned our trip for weeks. We had worked out how much water we needed, how much we could comfortably carry in our packs, how much food we would need and whether we could carry it, what should

RIGHT

In the desert, you must even be prepared for snow!

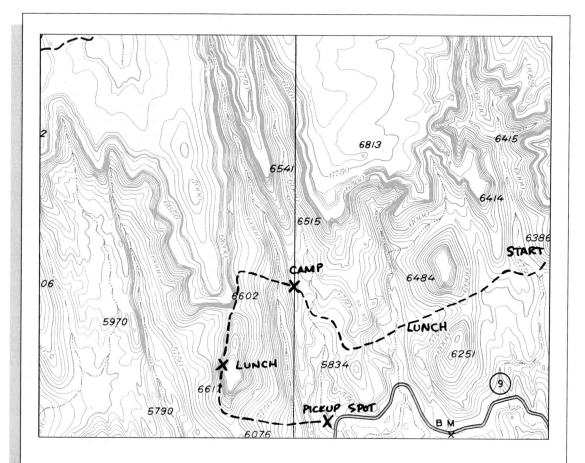

If this were your time-control plan, your trip might go something like this:

On the first day, you would hit the trail early in the morning, hiking four to five miles (about 7 km) before stopping for lunch. You could probably cover about the same distance in the afternoon, setting up camp at the base of a plateau just before supper.

The next morning, you would scramble up the plateau and have a late lunch at the top. Then you would descend and make your way to the pickup point, which you should have arranged with someone, by your designated time.

go in our first-aid kit, and what type of clothing would be necessary. Food, we had agreed, could not be skimped on. We were glad of that as we snuggled into our sleeping bags after a delicious pasta dinner.

T he next morning was bright and beautiful. Sunshine poured down onto a desert floor covered in — were our eyes deceiving us? — snow.

Time-control plans (TCPs)

In addition to helping you plan your trip, a TCP lets other people know where you plan to be at particular times. If you fail to return on time, they will then know where to start looking for you.

To write a TCP, check your route for trails, steep ground, and good camping places. Then plot your route and try to estimate how long each section will take. Don't forget that what looks like a short distance on the map may take a long time if the terrain is very steep or difficult. From your past hiking experience, you probably know how far you normally travel in an hour over various types of terrain. You may travel two miles (3.2 km) in 30 minutes on flat ground. Use your knowledge to plan the best route and schedule for you.

Anytime you plan a trip to the desert, think ahead. Try to find out what plants will help you if you run out of water. For instance, you could break off a piece of prickly pear (the cactus at right), singe it with matches, and brush off the spines (even the little furry ones) with a cloth. Then you would be able to suck liquid from the middle. You can also collect dew from plants in the early-morning hours.

ABOVE

Gaiters will keep your legs from becoming wet and scratched.

"Can you believe it snowed?" At least we would have plenty of water.

According to our topographical map, Fable Valley (which we were in) led to the base of the Dark Canyon Plateau. On the other side of that was Dark Canyon, which was where we wanted to be by the end of the day. After a quick breakfast of muesli, powdered milk mixed with water, and a hot drink, we started the long journey across the valley floor.

Warm weather and wet melting snow can seem deceptively easy for hiking. But fluffy clumps of white snow can hide small cacti and thorny bushes. The last thing we needed at the end of the day was cold wet feet and bleeding legs, so we put on our

Snow packed into a water bottle takes a long time to melt. Instead of drinking the last of your water and filling the bottle with snow, put some snow in while there's still water left. That way the snow will melt quickly and you will have a constant supply of water as long as you can find snow.

gaiters — leg coverings that reach from the tops of shoes to just below the knee — to protect our legs from the brush.

By the time we got to Dark Canyon Plateau, we were running low on drinking water. We were glad to find some unmelted snow to add to our water bottles. The long climb had left us very thirsty. The day was very sunny, so we put sunscreen on to keep from getting sunburned. We also hung bandanas from the backs of our hats to keep the sun off our necks. As we descended from the plateau into the canyon, heading for the road where Mary's brother would pick us up, I wished our trip would never end.

Never rely on finding water in the desert. Always bring enough along, even if it means packing less equipment. If you are short of water, you might be able to find some if you know what to look for. Make sure you purify any water you get from rivers, springs and streams before drinking it.

● *Look for trees. Some, such as cottonwoods, are near streams or springs that may have enough running water for you to collect.*
● *Walk uphill. You may find that you can see a stream.*
● *Collect dew from plants and rocks by wiping them with a small cloth. The cloth will eventually become saturated, and you can wring water out into a bottle.*
● *Eat non-poisonous plants, such as wild onions. You can also find liquid in cacti.*

MOUNTAINS

Hiking in the mountains, with your gear in a pack on your back, is one of the most satisfying activities in the world. Your group is independent; you have everything you need with you, so you can go miles from anywhere or anyone — into the most beautiful wilderness you can find.

You are also miles from anyone

A hiker, with a fully equipped pack, pauses before the beauty of the mountains at dusk.

who can help if you run into trouble. Never forget this. If you are in a secluded spot, people will have a difficult time reaching you to help out. So if you're going to get out of a tough situation, you will probably have to do it on your own. Remember this when you approach any trip, however short.

Ask yourself how you would cope in different situations. What would you do if a member of your group broke his or her ankle? How about if you get lost or separated, and the sun goes down while you are still miles from home? Or what if you find that the route you picked is too hard for some of the people in your group?

There are two keys to staying safe in the mountains. The most important is to think ahead and spot danger before someone is hurt. The second is to deal with problems that you hadn't spotted before they occurred. This second option is one you should try to avoid at all costs; if a dangerous situation becomes a very hazardous one, you have already begun to make mistakes that could prove costly.

Work as a group, not as individuals. If something does go wrong, three,

---

Equipment

For a safe day's mountain hiking, you should have:
- ✓ *daypack to hold your supplies*
- ✓ *waterproof coat that comes down past your hips*
- ✓ *warm sweater and long pants*
- ✓ *flashlight*
- ✓ *hat and gloves*
- ✓ **survival bag**
- ✓ *extra clothes*
- ✓ *first-aid kit*
- ✓ *extra food*
- ✓ *topographical map of the area and **orienteering compass***
- ✓ *emergency whistle*
- ✓ *water bottle filled with at least a quart of water*
- ✓ **hiking boots**
- ✓ *sunglasses*
- ✓ *waterproof matches*
- ✓ *pocketknife*

Remember that weather can change swiftly in the mountains. Always keep an eye out for approaching storms and seek shelter to stay safe, warm, and dry.

ABOVE

Companionship is
part of the fun of
an overnight trip.

four, or five people working as a team are more effective than the same number of people acting on their own.

Always keep the group together. There's a trick even to doing this, although it sounds easy. Some people walk faster than others. Make sure that the fast hikers don't get too far ahead of the slow ones. At least one fast hiker should stay at the back of the group to make sure the whole group stays at the pace of the slowest hiker. If the slowest hiker wants to rest, stop for a few minutes. Don't rest so long that you get cold, though.

The problem you are most likely to run into is someone getting injured. Twisted and sprained ankles are common hiking injuries. If the injury seems serious, someone should get help, and someone should stay with the injured hiker until help arrives. Never try to move anyone who is seriously injured. Just try to keep her or him warm and as comfortable as possible. Keep food and water close by, and get help as quickly as you can.

If you are in a large group, someone could easily become separated from

Hiking safely
means keeping
the group
together.

Packing a backpack

Organize your pack so you always know where things are. Pack food and water near the opening so you can reach them easily. Never pack fuel above food, because it will contaminate the food if the bottle leaks. Put similar things together in colored bags so that you only need to get hold of the clothes bag, for example, to find a new pair of socks. Try to put the softer things next to your back. Heavier items should also be near your back, at the center or top.

the others and get lost. Others may not realize one person is missing until much later. If this happens, stop immediately and begin a search.

The best way to conduct a search is to set up a central camp in a spot everyone can easily find. Two or three people should stay there. The others should pair up and head in different directions to look for the missing hiker. All pairs should return to the camp periodically to see if the missing person has turned up. If you can't find the hiker within a couple of hours, send one pair of hikers to get help

Bivouacking

In an emergency, **bivouacking** should keep you warm and alive, although you probably won't be very comfortable. Bivouacking is staying in a temporary shelter, like a survival bag.

If you get stuck on a mountain at night, you must work to keep yourself safe. Put on extra clothes, loosen your belt and boot laces to help your blood circulate, and slide into your survival bag. For extra warmth, you can gather twigs and leaves for a bed to give you insulation from the cold ground. Keep food and water nearby. If you get cold, get up and move around until you are warm again.

If you can't get warm, pair up into one survival bag for extra body heat.

Emergency whistle

Using a method of signaling with whistles when a hiker is lost may help you complete the search much sooner than walking and calling. Blow the whistle loudly six times. Wait one minute, then blow six times more. If the lost person hears the whistle, he or she should respond with three long blasts on the whistle.

BELOW

Hiking through the mountains in the dark is dangerous.

from a professional search-and-rescue team. The rest of your group should keep searching.

Once the search-and-rescue team is involved, listen to instructions, and make sure your group of hikers gets to safety before darkness falls. But notify the search-and-rescue team that you are safe, or they might spend valuable time looking for you as well as the missing person.

Potentially the most dangerous situation in the mountains is

Clothing

When you're in the mountains, the greatest danger isn't getting lost or injuring yourself, it's the cold. You must make sure your clothing will keep you dry and warm.

Dress in thin layers rather than thick layers. Adding or removing thin layers can make a big difference in controlling your body temperature. Avoid some natural fabrics, like cotton, that take a long time to dry. Waterproof clothing will keep you dry, and artificial insulation such as Thinsulate will keep you warm.

for your group to try hiking in the dark. Never hike through the mountains in the dark. Always make sure that you carry enough equipment so you can safely stay on the mountain until there is enough light to hike down.

Sometimes you will be faced with conditions for which the group isn't prepared. When this happens, you will have to find another route or go back the way you came. It would be impossible to list all the situations that might force you to retreat, but ask yourself the following questions when deciding whether to proceed over difficult ground:

● What is the terrain ahead? Is a slip likely? Would a slip result in an injury to someone?

● How well are the individuals in the group likely to cope with the difficult terrain? Are there inexperienced hikers in the group who are not very confident? They may be able to struggle through, but everyone must be able to cross easily for it to be safe.

● How much time do you have? You may be able to pick your way carefully over difficult ground, but will it take so long that you will be racing darkness to get to safety?

Whatever the situation, don't think that you have to act immediately. If you take the time to think through all the alternatives, you will probably make the right decision.

Your ultimate goal is to get everyone home safely, not to cover a certain number of miles or to complete a particular trail. If you must retreat, you can always try again later.

RIGHT

Exercise caution when going over difficult terrain.

RIVERS

In any dangerous sport, you must never go out alone. This is especially true of kayaking. Three is a minimum number, and four to six kayakers are ideal for a group. Always appoint someone to be the coordinator. The most important member of the group is the end paddler, because she or he will spot any problems the other kayakers are having and be in a position to help out. She or he is also the least likely to be spotted if something goes wrong. Because of this, the end paddler should be the most experienced kayaker.

Rivers can be very noisy, so kayakers use signals to tell each other things. Some signals are shown on the opposite page. You should use signals even if you can hear what other people are saying, so that when the noise of the river is deafening and you need them, you won't have forgotten what they are.

The key to safety on a river is using your past experience to guess what might be around the corner. If others

SIGNALS

Go that way

Stop

Continue

Something tricky ahead

in your group are more experienced than you, try to learn from them.

Never go kayaking without a life jacket securely fastened around your upper body. If you become separated from your kayak or, worse yet, knocked unconscious, it will help you stay afloat.

My friends Clare, George, and I had just finished a two-week kayaking course at the Rocky Mountain Outdoor Center in Howard, Colorado. We were eager to test our skills on an actual river trip. After carefully looking over the first major rapid on the river, we put our kayaks in the water and paddled off.

George entered the rapid first, disappeared for a moment, shot straight up in the air, and disappeared again. The next thing I knew, my boat was in a vertical dive, heading straight into a small **stopper** — a circulating undercurrent that sometimes traps kayaks. Fortunately, I had known the stopper was there, and I had thought about my options. I could allow my kayak to be sucked into the stopper or try to paddle through it. Paddling through looked like the best option, because it left me in control of where

I was going rather than at the mercy of the current.

I paddled like mad through the wall of white water in front of me, trying to keep up enough speed so that I wouldn't be sucked backwards. The bow of the kayak punched into the foaming water, and one desperate stroke later I popped out on the other side.

The rest of the rapid was a rollercoaster ride down to a patch of calm water. I found George waiting there for me, and Clare arrived soon afterward. We agreed that the best thing we had done was to scout out the rapid before kayaking it, so that we were ready for the stopper.

W e had already picked out three possible camping places on the map, and we decided to see what they were like. The first was terrible — we didn't even have to get out of our boats to see that we couldn't sleep on a pile of boulders. A half mile of paddling brought us around a bend and into sight of a sandy beach, grass and trees. This was the place for us!

We pulled our boats out of the water and tied them to a tree so that they couldn't be pulled off the beach

by the current. George heated up water, and Clare and I peeled off our clammy **wetsuits** and put on some warm, dry clothes. Then we sat in our sleeping bags and sipped steaming hot chocolate. I fell asleep exhausted but happy.

We had a great time that day and on the trip that followed because we were well prepared. In any dangerous sport, the first thing to do to ensure your survival is to be prepared for anything that might happen.

Advance planning of our route and our camping spots, the right equipment, and fit bodies that were up to the adventure all helped to make sure the trip was a success.

When kayaking through dangerous sections of the river, you must keep paddling. Otherwise you may lose control of your direction and wind up being dragged wherever the river wants to take you. This could be into a stopper, down a waterfall, into rocks, or into any of a hundred other dangerous situations. Your arms and shoulders are the driving force of your boat, so make sure they are fit. Swimming is an ideal way to strengthen your arms

ABOVE

A perfect camping spot alongside the river.

27

and upper body. Pull-ups and push-ups are also useful training exercises.

One of the most important self-rescue techniques in kayaking is getting out of the kayak if it capsizes.

Before you head into dangerous water, you should practice **wet exits** until you are confident that you can escape an overturned kayak in an emergency. Kayaks have **spray**

decks that fit over your torso and seal the opening of the kayak to keep water out of the cockpit. When performing a wet exit, you must release the spray deck by pulling on the grab loop in front of you and detaching the spray deck from the kayak. (All spray decks should have a release cord. If yours doesn't, don't use it.) This should free you from the kayak, so you can simply push it away and float to the surface.

There are ways of righting an overturned kayak without making a wet exit, although you should not hesitate to make a wet exit if you sense any danger. Sometimes you can get help from nearby kayakers by using a distress signal (such as banging on the sides of the kayak three times). By running your hands alongside the kayak between distress signals, you will find the other kayak when it bumps into yours. Grab it and use it to right yourself. You might also try righting yourself with your paddle.

Most importantly, don't panic if you get into a tricky situation. If you stay calm and remember your training, you have a good chance of coming out safely. If you panic, you could get yourself into even more danger.

Once you have made a wet exit from your boat, you could well be in fast-flowing water some distance

RIGHT

If you fall out, hold onto the end of your kayak while you catch your breath and think about how to rescue yourself.

from the bank. What do you do? Stay with your kayak while you get your breath back. Make sure you are on the upstream side of your kayak, and hold on to the bow or stern to lessen the chances of it getting caught in rocks or fallen trees. If you can see that you are approaching a rapid or congested section of the river, swim away from the kayak.

If you are without your kayak, always float on your back and look at your feet — even if you're trying to swim. This type of swimming stroke will help you conserve energy. It will

BELOW

These kayakers have managed to get themselves and their kayak to the bank safely.

THE WET EXIT

Stay calm when the kayak overturns.

Release the spray deck by pulling on the grab loop in front of you.

Roll forward out of the kayak, then push it out of your way.

also keep your head out of the water and increase your visibility to other kayakers.

The best option if you have fallen into the water is to save yourself by swimming to the bank, without relying on other people. Decide which bank you can safely reach and swim steadily for it. Don't use up all your strength at once, because it could take a while to get there.

If you can't get out at the bank for some reason (because the bank is too steep, for example), you will have to rely on other people for a rescue. At some point someone might throw you a rope. To catch the rope, spread out your arms and legs to make yourself a larger target. When the line hits you, grab it with both hands, pull it to your chest, and wrap it over one

shoulder. Then your rescuer can pull you to the bank.

I f the river current is very strong, a rescuer will find throwing a rope practically fruitless. You will be moving too fast. Another kayak may be your only source of help.

Foremost, the other kayaker must be able to reach you. When he or she does, you must be prepared to help as much as possible. The rescuer should approach you from downstream and try to position the kayak so you will hit it just behind the cockpit. Hold on to the rear grab handle and rest for as long as you need, then pull yourself up onto the back of the kayak. Keep your legs positioned wide apart for stability.

Don't try to rescue others this way, unless you have no other choice and unless you are very experienced. You may end up in the water as well.

The best safety precaution you can take is to enroll in a kayaking class before going out on the river. Make sure you learn all the techniques properly, and practice them again and again in a swimming pool or calm, shallow water before getting into rough water.

BELOW

In a fast-flowing river like this one, you may not be able to get out at the riverbank. Instead, you may have to rely on others for help.

THE BEACH

There's nothing better than spending a hot, lazy day on the beach. If you get too hot in the sunshine, you can always cool off in the water. When you get hungry or thirsty, you can always find some shade and have a picnic lunch or an ice-cold beverage. All around, there's the smell of suntan lotion and the sound of people having fun. Danger seems miles away.

But danger is as close as the water. If you are a surfer, windsurfer, or skin diver, you probably already understand the dangers of the ocean. Waves can submerge you, and currents can quickly drag you far from the shore. Speedboats and yachts are just as dangerous, because they may run you over if their drivers fail to see you. You need to be aware of all the dangers and

practice proper safety to reduce your risk of being hurt.

When you get to the beach, look around carefully. Are people swimming? If not, find out why. They may be staying away from the water because of dangerous currents or water pollution. Ask someone very familiar with the beach to explain what hazards you should watch for. If you are at a swimming beach, see if a lifeguard is on duty before you enter the water.

If the water is rough, don't go in unless you are a strong swimmer.

Help!

If you fall out of a boat and cannot swim to shore, or if you have gotten too far away from the shore to safely return, what should you do? If you were in a boat, you should have been wearing a life jacket that will keep you afloat. You will be able to wave your arms in the air, back and forth across each other. This is generally recognized as a signal for help.

If you aren't wearing a life jacket, cup your hands and splash the surface layer of water away from you as hard as you can. The spray from this can go high into the air and is quite easy to see, especially if it catches the sunlight.

If you do find yourself caught in a current, don't panic. Relax. Let yourself float for a while and work out where the current is taking you. Then swim with the current, but angle yourself toward the shoreward edge of it. The trick is to get out of the current with enough energy left to allow you to get back to shore. Never try to fight the current by swimming against it. This is impossible, and you will exhaust yourself very quickly. Remember: Get out of the current, then get back to safety.

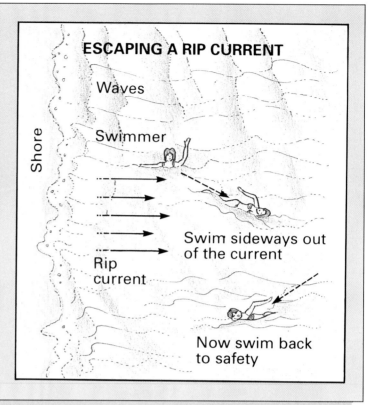

ESCAPING A RIP CURRENT

Waves

Shore

Swimmer

Swim sideways out of the current

Rip current

Now swim back to safety

Even if the water seems calm, don't go into deep water if you don't swim very well. If you can't swim, don't go into the ocean at all, even on a water mattress. Water mattresses can easily be blown out to sea, and they can deflate if they are punctured.

Nearly all the people who lifeguards rescue have gotten caught in a **rip current**. Rip currents travel away from the shore on the surface of the ocean, and they can easily pull swimmers out to sea. Being in a rip current can be scary for anyone, but it's even more terrifying for people who don't swim well.

L earn to spot rip currents — narrow flows of water heading to sea — before you get caught in them. "Rips" are caused by waves, tides, the water bottom, and the shoreline. Because they are so strong, rip currents stir up a lot of sand and plant material from the water bottom. One way to spot a rip is to watch for murky water. The surfaces of rips are also relatively waveless, although

ABOVE

Even if you are a very strong swimmer, avoid waves like these.

they will have ripples because of the water movement. Sometimes rip currents are the calm water between two areas with breaking waves.

Rip currents happen because water must return to the sea after being swept to shore by a wave. The water cannot travel against the powerful waves pushing even more water in, so it flows along the shore until it reaches an area without waves. From there, the water heads swiftly out to sea in a strong, narrow channel. Surfers, scuba divers, and

Live dangers

Whenever you are visiting an ocean beach, look out for dangerous sea creatures. Sea urchins are found on rocky coastlines of Europe, North America, and the Mediterranean Sea. Both sea urchins and jellyfish can leave you with a nasty sting if you touch them. Sharks sometimes attack people near the shore. Consult local beach fanatics to find out what dangers exist.

windsurfers sometimes use rip currents to move quickly away from shore. However, rip currents are dangerous for swimmers, and no one should enter a rip current without plenty of experience.

Water traveling along the shore to get to a rip current, or from waves approaching the shore at an angle, can create **longshore currents** that are also dangerous for swimmers.

If you get caught in any kind of current, don't panic. You will exhaust yourself quickly if you try swimming against the current. The safest way to get out of a current is to swim steadily in the direction that it is taking you, but toward the closest edge of the current. Work with it until you escape, then swim to shore. If the effort leaves you exhausted, flip onto your back and float toward the shore until you regain

BELOW

Avoid areas of calm water like the one you can see between two sets of waves. They may hide a rip current!

Rip currents also
form beside solid
objects like piers.

energy. The waves may also help
push you inward.

You must also be careful when
walking on the beach. The
waves often wash up garbage and
pollutants that have been dumped or
spilled into the ocean, along with other
debris. If you walk recklessly while
barefoot, or even in tongs, you are
risking cuts and puncture wounds.
The waves also wash up sea urchins
and other ocean life-forms. Avoid
touching these, because many can
give you a painful sting.

Swimming safety

*Don't dive headfirst into
shallow water. You can
break your neck and
become paralyzed if you hit
your head on the bottom or
another object you haven't
seen. Always check out the
water bottom by walking on
it and looking for potential
hazards.*

THE CITY

We often think of survival in terms of the wilderness, but very few of us actually live in the wilderness. Most of us live in cities or towns, where the real danger comes from other people rather than dangerous conditions. You can still apply the same basic principles to urban survival as you would to wilderness survival. Look ahead and try to spot problems before they happen. If you do find yourself in trouble, keep a clear head and get out of it as quickly and safely as possible.

What would you do if you found youself in a city where you didn't know anyone and you had no money? Would you know how to get help? If one person failed to help, would you be discouraged? This story will help you to consider what you might do in similar circumstances. Would you have done anything differently?

LEFT and RIGHT

Large cities can
be terrifying,
especially at night.
You must
constantly be
aware of your
surroundings.

When my bus arrived at Manchester, England, I was stuck there. A bus drivers' strike had disrupted the schedules, and I was only partway home from a wilderness camp in Scotland. I called home to tell my parents where I was, and I managed only to get the answering machine. I left a message telling them what had happened.

I stood in a long line of angry passengers and was eventually told that the next bus to London was in eight hours. I asked if there was somewhere to wait and was directed toward a line of seats. I guess the woman I asked thought I looked old enough to take care of myself.

I piled my backpack and another gear bag onto a cart and sat down. At least I would have a chance to finish my book! I was reading the last chapter when I heard a man's voice behind me.

"Mind if I join you?" Before I could answer, a well-dressed man sat down in the seat next to me.

"Traveling on your own?" he asked.

> **Valuables**
>
> *Never keep all of your valuables in the same place. If all your money and travel papers are in the same bag, one theft could wipe you out. By placing some of your valuables in your fanny pack, carrying some in your backpack, and leaving some where you are staying, you won't lose them all at once.*

BELOW

At a train station in Barcelona, Spain, people await their boarding calls.

"No," I said, and looked away.

"You don't have to be so rude. I'm not going to hurt you. Here, my name's Alexander, what's yours?" He held out his hand. I was almost embarrassed to shake hands with him, my hands were so calloused and rough. Had I really been rude? What would my mother think of me?

"Hi," I managed to say.

"Can I buy you a drink?"

"I'm too young to drink," I replied, closing my book.

Always stay where you can be seen. During the day, make sure there are other people around. At night stay where there is good lighting. Keep an eye open for telephones, and never be afraid to dial 911 and ask for help.

"You look very grown up for your age then. Hey, you look like the adventurous type. How would you like me to drive you home in my Porsche?"

"But I live in London. It's hundreds of kilometers away." The adventurous part of me was saying, *Go on, you've never been in a Porsche before. It'll be OK.*

"No problem. That's exactly where I'm heading. Let's go," Alexander said, standing up.

"I can't leave my gear here," I said. Just for a moment he looked very annoyed, but then the look was gone, and I thought I must have imagined it.

"No problem, there's room in the boot [trunk] for it." That was when I began to get very suspicious. Porsches don't have trunks that big.

Always tell your family and friends where you are going to be and what time you will be home. If you change your plans, leave word at home. Stay aware of what is happening around you. If you think you are in danger, get help by going into a store or office and calling the police.

Traveling checklist

✓ *money for food and emergencies*
✓ *somewhere to stay*
✓ *map of the city*
✓ *telephone numbers of people to call for help*
✓ *experienced guide, if possible*
✓ *whistle to signal for help*

ABOVE

Avoid subway stations, like this one in New York, especially when there are few other people around.

My gear had filled up my mother's station wagon.

"OK," I said, "but I have to go to the toilet first. Wait here."

I shouldn't have let him talk to me at all. I should have yelled for help when he wouldn't go away. Loud noise always draws attention in public places, and people doing something wrong hate being watched.

I saw a woman with two children and ran up to her.

Places to avoid

In any city, there are places you should avoid, especially at night. Subway stations, bus depots, alleys, and parking ramps are often deserted at night, leaving you vulnerable to attack. Stay away from narrow streets that are badly lit, because muggers can easily hide in the shadows. While you are walking, look as though you know where you are going and are confident. If you look nervous, thieves and assailants are more likely to target you.

ABOVE

If you travel with other people, you are less likely to attract unwanted attention.

"Help. There's a guy over there trying to make me leave with him." She looked startled at first, but then she told another stranger, who had the courage to holler "Police!" as loud as she could.

Alexander was heading for the exit when he was caught. He turned out to be a prime suspect in crimes against children. There are other people out there who are like Alexander. If you run into someone who makes you extremely uncomfortable, won't leave you alone, or tries to get you to go with them,

● *Never approach a car to give directions. If you get too close, someone could easily grab you and pull you in, or another person could come up from behind and shove you into the car.*

● *Listen to your intuition and don't be afraid to make noise. It's much better to make a scene and be safe 24 hours later than to risk being attacked, kidnapped, or robbed.*

● *Whenever you can, travel with people you know. You are much less likely to attract attention if you are in a group than if you are on your own.*

don't be embarrassed to shout for help. Don't second-guess yourself. Embarrassing someone is better than risking your life.

Glossary

Bivouacking Camping overnight with a makeshift shelter, such as a survival bag or an enclosure made from a tent. People who bivouac usually do not plan on staying out overnight, but are prepared to do so when circumstances, such as darkness, keep them from getting back to safety.

Campsite A place where you pitch a tent. Some parks have official campsites and do not allow people to camp elsewhere in the park without special permission. Many official campsites have showers and fire pits for cooking.

Carabiner An oval-shaped, metal ring with a snap link. Carabiners are used most often in climbing, but they have uses for other sports. Kayakers use carabiners to attach loops (to form grab handles) to their kayaks.

First aid Minor treatment given to an injured person; also the lifesaving treatment given a seriously injured person while waiting for medical help

Hiking boots Special boots, made of leather or fabric, that are designed for hiking. These boots give ample support to the parts of the feet that are stressed by hiking. The soles of hiking boots are designed for maximum traction.

Gaiters A cloth or leather covering for the lower part of the leg

Longshore current A channel of fast-moving water that travels parallel to the shore. These currents usually feed into a rip current bringing water washed onto shore back out to sea.

Orienteering compass A compass that has a base plate with a "direction-of-travel" arrow and a rotating housing that allows you to make adjustments as necessary for your map. Orienteering compasses not only tell you in what direction you are traveling, but allow you to determine which way to travel in order to get to a certain place on the map.

Rip current Fast-moving channels of deep water heading out to sea from the shore. These currents are so strong that they will carry swimmers far from the shore very quickly.

Sling A loop of rope or tubular webbing that has many uses. Kayakers use them to form grab handles on their kayaks and as tie lines to secure the kayak to a dock or some other stationary object when it is not being used.

Spray deck A piece of waterproof material that forms a seal between your body and the opening of a kayak. Spray decks fit tightly over your torso and attach to the kayak so water can't get into the cockpit.

Stopper A circulating undercurrent that sometimes forms in river rapids. A kayak that gets caught in a stopper will have to fight the opposing forces of the stopper, which is pushing the kayak backward, and the rapids, which are pushing the kayak forward.

Survival bag   A lightweight, waterproof bag that can fit over a sleeping bag to keep it dry. Survival bags can also be used alone, in an emergency, to keep someone warm.

Time-control plan   A plan, usually drawn on a topographical map, showing the route, the estimated time for traveling specific sections, and stopping places along the way

Topographical map   A map that shows the surface features, such as hills, trees, rivers, and trails, of an area

Wet exit   A method of getting out of an overturned kayak. Wet exits involve removing the spray deck, rolling forward out of the cockpit, and pushing the kayak out of the way so you can get to the surface.

Wetsuit   An article of clothing that is designed to keep you warm in cold water. Wetsuits come in all styles, sizes, and colors. They are usually made of a fabric that allows water to pass through to your skin, but which provides a great deal of insulation to trap your body heat.

White-water kayaking   Maneuvering a kayak over rapids that flow fast and pass over obstacles so that the water appears white

Books

Armstrong, Wayne. *Camping Basics.* Englewood Cliffs, New Jersey: Prentice-Hall, 1985.

Axcell, Claudia. *Simple Foods for the Pack: The Sierra Club Guide to Delicious Natural Foods for the Trail.* New York, New York: Random House, 1986.

Fieldbook. Irving, Texas: Boy Scouts of America, 1984.

Foster, Lynne. *Take a Hike! The Sierra Club Kid's Guide to Hiking and Backpacking.* Boston, Massachusetts: Little Brown, 1991.

Freeman, Tony. *Beginning Backpacking.* Chicago, Illinois: Children's Press, 1980.

Ganci, David. *Desert Hiking.* Berkley, California: Wilderness Press, 1988.

Jacobson, Cliff. *Camping Secrets.* Merrillville, Indiana: ICS Books, 1987.

———. *The Basic Essentials of Map and Compass.* Merrillville, Indiana: ICS Books, 1987.

McManus, Patrick F. *Kid Camping from Aaaii! to Zip.* New York, New York, Lothrup, 1979.

McVey, Vicki. *The Sierra Club Wayfinding Book.* Boston, Massachusetts: Little Brown, 1989.

Moran, Tom. *Canoeing is for Me.* Minneapolis, Minnesota: Lerner Publications, 1984.

Olsen, Larry. *Outdoor Survival Skills.* Chicago, Illinois: Chicago Review, 1990.

Sanders, Pete. *Safety Guide: Outdoors.* New York, New York: Aladdin Books, 1989.

Thomas, Art. *Backpacking is for Me.* Minneapolis, Minnesota: Lerner Publications, 1980.

Videos

Finding Your Way in the Wild. Minneapolis, Minnesota: Quality Video, 1990.

Backpacking America. Luther, Oklahoma: Harrison and Company, 1986.

More information

American Camping Association
5000 State Road, 67N
Martinsville, Indiana 46151 USA

American Canoe Association
P.O. Box 1190
Newington, Virginia 22122 USA

American Hiking Society
1015 31st Street Northwest
Washington, D.C. 20007 USA

Future Advancement of Camping
P.O. Box 8
Hatteras, North Carolina 27943 USA

The Mountaineers
300 Third Avenue West
Seattle, Washington 98119 USA

National Campers and Hikers Association
4808 Transist Road, Building 2
Depew, New York 14043 USA

Outdoor Education Association
143 Fox Hill Road
Denville, New Jersey 07834 USA

The Sierra Club
730 Polk Street
San Francisco, California 94115 USA

U.S. Canoe Association
606 Ross Street
Middletown, Ohio 45044 USA

Wilderness Education Association
20 Winona Avenue, Box 39
Saranac Lake, New York 12983 USA

Index

613.6
ROB

Roberts, Libby

Survival skills